MW00890822

LILA THE LADYBUG

A Deep Creek Lake Adventure

By Cindy Freland
and Anne Davidson

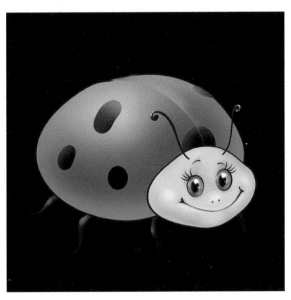

Copyright © 2016 by Cindy Freland and Anne Davidson

All rights reserved. No part of this publication may be reproduced, distributed, or transmitted in any form or by any means, including photocopying, recording, or other electronic or mechanical methods, without the prior written permission of the publisher, except in the case of brief quotations embodied in critical reviews and certain other noncommercial uses permitted by copyright law. For permission requests, contact the author, by email at cindy@marylandsecretarial.com, or by phone at (301) 352-7927.

Printed in the United States of America.

DEDICATION

To my daughters, Alyssa and Andrea,

who inspire me every day. I love YOU!

~ Cindy Freland

To our family who has supported our crazy

lavender adventure from the beginning.

~ Anne Davidson

Lila the Ladybug was born to loving parents.
She was happy living with her mom, dad,
brother, Billy, and sister, Iris.

They lived in the garden near a popular farm in Accident, Maryland. The garden had flowering herbs, including dill, fennel, and cilantro, for cooking. It also had gorgeous, brightly colored zinnias, asters, and sunflowers.

Lila knew she was loved but she also knew she was different. Her mom called her "Lila, my little Lavender Ladybird." Ladybird is another name for ladybug.

Lila was a beautiful shade of lavender, not the bright red like the rest of her family. She had a pink face and a happy smile.

Some of the other ladybugs teased Lila. They said, "We don't want to play with you. You don't look like us."

Because of her special color, Lila wasn't allowed to play outside with friends and siblings.

The red color of ladybugs keeps them safe from birds and other predators. It tells predators that the ladybugs may not taste very good.

"Lila, your lavender color looks delicious! Birds, frogs, wasps, spiders, and dragonflies may think you're a tasty treat. You must stay close to home for your protection. I'm sorry but a mother's job is to keep her children safe from harm," said Lila's mom.

Lila was miserable. Her brother and sister would try to cheer Lila up by telling her about the exciting places they visited and the adventures they experienced. But it only made Lila more miserable.

All she wanted to do was play
with her friends and siblings.
She loved eating aphids,
which are garden pests.

Billy and Iris were sad, too. They missed playing with their sister. Before they knew of the danger to Lila, the three would spend the day chasing each other and playing wonderful games.

Lila dreamed of the perfect place where she would fit in. It would be a place, a Lavender Ladybird place, where she wouldn't be teased because of her special color.

Billy and Iris loved visiting the flowers on the farms and gardens near Deep Creek Lake. The air was fresh and there were always lots of happy children.

One day, Billy and Iris returned from one of their flying adventures with exciting news. They had found a wonderful place in the Allegheny Mountains of western Maryland, called **Deep Creek Lavender Farm.**

Deep Creek
Lavender
Farm

Deep Creek Lavender Farm had lots and lots of lavender plants in purple, white and pink. What a gorgeous, fragrant place to live.

Everywhere they looked they saw the beautiful color of Lila... lavender! Lila would blend right in. The birds and other predators would never spot her. The lavender was beautiful and the scent made Billy and Iris happy. This was the perfect place for Lila!

Mom and Dad Ladybug flew out the very next day to Deep Creek Lavender Farm. They had to agree with Billy and Iris, this farm was the perfect place for the family and their special Lavender Ladybird, Lila.

As the sun began to set and darkness fell, the Ladybug family, Lila included, flew to Deep Creek Lavender Farm where Lila blended in with the beautiful lavender and was safe.

LADYBIRD, LADYBIRD

The ladybird was immortalized in the popular children's nursery rhyme *Ladybird, Ladybird*:

Ladybird, ladybird, fly away home.

Your house is on fire and your children are gone.

All except one, and that's Little Anne,

For she has crept under the frying pan.

There has been some speculation that this nursery rhyme originates from the time of the **Great Fire of London** in 1666.

FACTS ABOUT LADYBUGS

- The Coccinellidae are in the insect family of small beetles, ranging from .0315 to .708 inches.

- They are commonly yellow, orange, or red with small black spots on their wing covers, with black legs, heads, and antennae.

- Coccinellids are found worldwide, with over 5,000 species.

- They are known as ladybugs in North America, and ladybirds in other areas.

- Entomologists, scientists who study insects, in the United States widely prefer the names ladybird beetles or lady beetles as these insects are not true bugs.

- Ladybugs are considered useful insects because many species feed on aphids, whiteflies, thrips, spider mites, and scale, which are garden pests.

- They often are among the first insects to appear in the spring.

- Their average life span is one to two years.

- Each ladybug eats up to 80 aphids per day.

- Ladybugs won't harm people, plants, or pets and can assist with pollination in areas where bee populations have decreased.

- Besides the prey, most ladybugs eat honeydew, pollen, plant sap, nectar, and various fungi.

- Flowers that attract ladybugs have umbrella shaped flowers such as fennel, dill, cilantro, caraway, angelica, tansy, wild carrot, and yarrow.

- Apart from planting attractive plants in the garden, you can also promote ladybug populations by eliminating insecticides.

- The predators of ladybugs are birds, frogs, wasps, spiders, and dragonflies.

- The bright colors of many coccinellids discourage some potential predators from making a meal of them. This phenomenon works because predators learn by experience to associate certain prey colors with a bad taste.

- When disturbed, they may secrete an odorous, distasteful fluid from their joints to discourage enemies.

- Ladybugs are the official state insect of Delaware, Massachusetts, New Hampshire, Ohio, and Tennessee.

- The spotted wing covers on ladybugs are made from a material called chitin, the same material as our fingernails.

- Many cultures consider ladybugs lucky and have nursery rhymes or local names for the insects. The people of Russia, Turkey, and Italy think the ladybug is either a reason to make a wish or a sign that a wish will soon come true.

- Despite her legal name of "Claudia," Mrs. Johnson, wife of President Lyndon B. Johnson, has been known as "Lady Bird" since childhood, when her nursemaid, Alice Tittle, commented that she was "as purty as a lady bird."

ATTRACTING LADYBUGS

Hummingbirds, butterflies and ladybugs are just a few of our pollinators. They spread pollen from one plant to another, causing flowers to bloom and trees and bushes to form fruit, while being an enjoyable source of entertainment. It is easy to lure hummingbirds, butterflies and ladybugs to gardens by choosing colorful and nectar-rich plants. Beebalm, butterfly bushes and cornflowers are easy to grow and known to attract these beneficial pollinators.

Hummingbirds, butterflies and ladybugs are attracted to three things: food, blooms and colors. When planning your pollinator garden, consider flowers rich with nectar and pollen. Nectar provides food that fast-moving hummingbirds and butterflies require and ladybugs will eat pollen as a source of protein in addition to devouring pests like aphids. Flower structure matters and tubular petals are ideal receptacles for hummingbirds to hover over and collect pollen while butterflies and ladybugs require open flowers where they can land. Bright colors attract pollinators and the most attractive colors are orange, yellow, white and purple. Whenever possible, choose native plants which require less maintenance and are most appropriate for the needs of local wildlife.

HOW THE LADYBUG GOT ITS NAME

Legends vary about how the Ladybug came to be named, but the most common (and enduring) is this: In Europe, during the Middle Ages, swarms of insects were destroying the crops. The farmers prayed to the Virgin Mary for help. Soon thereafter the Ladybugs came, devouring the plant-destroying pests and saving the crops! The farmers called these beautiful insects "The Beetles of Our Lady", and, over time, they eventually became popularly known as "Lady Beetles." The red wings were said to represent the Virgin's cloak and the black spots were symbolic of both her joys and her sorrows.

BOOKS WRITTEN BY CINDY FRELAND

You will find the following books written by Cindy Freland on Amazon.com:

Pond Adventures with Aragon
Felix and the Purple Giant
Easy Guide to Your Facebook Business Page
Get a Job! Your Resume and Interview Guide
Monkey Farts: A Guide to Selling Your Handmade Crafts and Direct Sales Products
Easy and Free Self-Publishing: A Guide to Getting Your Book in Print and Kindle on Amazon
An American Virtual Assistant: The "Good, Bad and Ugly of Owning a Business Support Service
You Might Be Surprised: Marketing Ideas to Help Grow Your Business
Mud Pies
No More Excuses: How to start a profitable business from your home on a shoestring budget
Jordan the Jellyfish: A Chesapeake Bay Adventure
Curtis the Crab: A Chesapeake Bay Adventure
Heather the Honey Bee: A Chesapeake Bay Adventure
Oakley the Oyster: A Chesapeake Bay Adventure
Olivia the Osprey: A Chesapeake Bay Adventure
Vandi the Garden Fairy
Also please check out www.cbaykidsbooks.com.

Co-Author:
Cindy Freland

Cindy Freland's inspiration comes from her love of children and animals. Most of her children's books are based on true events. Her passion is teaching children about the beauty and the bounty of the Chesapeake Bay. She has written many children's and business books with many more children's books coming soon, including Christmas with Marco, Paisley the Pony, and Chester the Chipmunk. Her books can be purchased on www.cbaykidsbooks.com and www.amazon.com. Freland lives in Bowie, Maryland, with her family and dog, Juno.

Co-Author:
Anne Davidson

Anne Davidson and her husband, Scott, opened Deep Creek Lavender Farm in 2013. Located in Accident, Maryland, the farm has two thousand lavender plants blooming in colors of purple, lavender, white and pink. Growing in small steps year after year, the farm now has a barn store, chickens, cutting flowers and more and is open to visitors throughout the summer. Anne believes the farm's success is dependent on taking it one step at a time. Lila the Ladybug, A Deep Creek Lake Adventure, is Anne's first children's book with Cindy Freland, but more adventures for Lila are planned. Anne and Scott have two grown children and are founding members of the US Lavender Growers Association.

www.DeepCreekLavenderFarm.com

Illustrator: Sudipta Steve Dasgupta

I'm Sudipta Dasgupta, AKA Steve, in the arena of artworks - born to do illustration alongside my passion for painting. I severed ties with the dreaded curricula of my science courses in some forlorn time. I shook hands with the dream that I always dreamed - to become an artist and to do my work every minute, every hour of my life. I ensured my life would take this course for today, tomorrow and for all time to come. My passion is my profession. I enjoy creating all forms of illustration while staying true to my love of painting as well. I live in Kolkata, India but I mainly work for clients in the United States. I also illustrated Paisley the Pony: An Assateague Island Adventure, for Cindy Freland. www.dasguptarts.com

CPSIA information can be obtained
at www.ICGtesting.com
Printed in the USA
BVIC01n0201081016
464104BV00002B/6

9 781941 927960